Sometimes I Feel
FRUSTRATED

Published by Inhabit Education | www.inhabiteducation.com

Inhabit Education (Iqaluit), P.O. Box 2129, Iqaluit, Nunavut, X0A 1H0
(Toronto), 191 Eglinton Avenue East, Suite 301, Toronto, Ontario, M4P 1K1

Design and layout copyright © 2018 Inhabit Education
Text copyright © Inhabit Education
Illustrations by Amanda Sandland © Inhabit Education
Character design by Ali Hinch © Inhabit Education

All rights reserved. The use of any part of this publication reproduced,
transmitted in any form or by any means, electronic, mechanical, photocopying,
recording, or otherwise, or stored in a retrievable system, without written
consent of the publisher, is an infringement of copyright law.

Printed in Canada.

ISBN: 978-1-77266-885-8

INHABIT
EDUCATION

Today was the first day of school!
Tiu-tiu was excited to start a new grade.
She had loved school last year. She
couldn't wait to see her classmates and
meet her new teacher.

Tiu-tiu found her friend Vivi on the playground. Vivi had been her best friend at school last year.

"Let's walk to our new classroom together!" Tiu-tiu said.

Inside their classroom, they found their desks. They were going to sit next to each other all year!

"I'm so happy we can sit together!" Vivi said, smiling at Tiu-tiu.

Their teacher asked the class if they would like to share what they did that summer.

Tiu-tiu remembered doing this last year. It was so fun to hear everyone's stories about camping and travelling and playing in town.

Then the teacher asked Tiu-tiu, Vivi, and some other students to sit together in a group. They were going to try reading out loud as a group. Each student would read a sentence from the book.

Tiu-tiu wasn't used to reading out loud.

When it was her turn, Tiu-tiu needed a lot of help from her teacher. She had trouble reading one word, then another.

Tiu-tiu felt frustrated. Her face felt hot and she couldn't focus on the words in the book.

"Why can't our teacher read to us?"
Tiu-tiu asked Vivi.

"If our teacher reads to us all the time,
we won't learn to read on our own,"
Vivi said. "It's okay to make mistakes.
Practice will help you get better!"

Tiu-tiu wasn't so sure.

Soon it was time for math class. The teacher started drawing shapes on the board. Vivi seemed to know the names of all the shapes. Tiu-tiu was frustrated that she couldn't remember anything from last year!

"How do you know all these shapes?" Tiu-tiu asked.

Now Tiu-tiu felt frustrated with Vivi. How did he know everything? They were in the same class together last year and learned all the same things!

"We learned about these shapes last year," Vivi replied. "If you take your time, you will remember the names too! I can help you!"

"I don't need your help!" Tiu-tiu said. She scowled and turned her back to Vivi.

At recess, Tiu-tiu wouldn't talk to Vivi. Instead, she sat all by herself. She was so frustrated that she felt like she might cry.

Her friends Uka and Nauka walked over to her.

"What's wrong, Tiu-tiu?" Uka asked.

"I don't like school this year," Tiu-tiu told her friends. "I'm bad at everything!"

"But Tiu-tiu, you are good at lots of things!" Nauka said and smiled.

"Yeah!" Uka said, hopping up and down. "Remember how good you are at drawing?"

Tiu-tiu loved art class. She was excited to learn how to draw new animals.

"Everyone is good at something," Nauka said. "And we can all help each other learn new things!"

Tiu-tiu knew that Nauka was right. Now she felt badly about being mean to Vivi.

Tiu-tiu flew to find Vivi on the playground.

"Vivi, I'm sorry I was mean to you earlier," Tiu-tiu said. "I was frustrated. You are so good at reading and math. Those subjects are hard for me."

Vivi smiled slowly.

"I know, Tiu-tiu," Vivi said. "Sometimes I get frustrated when I'm trying to learn something new, too!"

Tiu-tiu put her arm around Vivi.

"Maybe we can help each other learn new things from now on!" Tiu-tiu said.

"I'd like that," Vivi said. "Art class is next! Will you teach me how to draw a polar bear?"

Tiu-tiu smiled. She was happy to help someone learn something new.